Falling Again

A Sweet Romance

Paula Kay

Copyright © 2023 by Paula Kay

All rights reserved.

No part of this book may be reproduced in any form or by any electronic or mechanical means, including information storage and retrieval systems, without written permission from the author, except for the use of brief quotations in a book review.

Cover designed by GetCovers

❀ Created with Vellum

Contents

1. Janet — 1
2. Janet — 8
3. Rick — 16
4. Janet — 25
5. Rick — 32
6. Janet — 37
7. Rick — 44
8. Janet — 49
9. Rick – 6 Months Later — 55

Chapter 1

Janet

This was it. She was going to do it. Now or never, do or die, or whatever.

She was going to tell him how she felt.

"I, Janet Meyers, am a strong, independent woman," she mumbled under her breath, hyping herself up. "I take charge, I kick butt, and I don't wait for the guy to make the first move."

Despite her little pep talk, though, her feet remained rooted in place. She was standing on the back patio, staring out over her family's backyard where a crowd of people had gathered for barbecue, drinks, and farewells. At the center of the party was her brother, Evan, and his best friend, Rick Masters.

Tall, dark, and handsome barely began to scratch the surface when it came to Rick. With his black hair and dark blue eyes, he looked like he could be the antihero in some teenage drama on the CW. He was the exact opposite of Evan in both looks and demeanor. Evan was a red-blonde extrovert with bright green eyes that crinkled in the corners when he smiled...and he smiled a lot. On the other hand, Rick was aloof and broody. He didn't try to claim the spotlight, it just always seemed to find him.

He was beautiful.

Cool.

Unattainable.

And Janet was completely in love with him.

As she stood there, building up the courage to go over and talk to him, her dad suddenly shouted for everyone's attention so he could give a speech.

As all eyes turned to him, Janet realized the opportunity this presented to her. She left the porch and slipped into the crowd, easing her way closer to Rick, unnoticed.

"I just want to thank everyone for coming today to send off our boys," her dad declared as she tiptoed around one person after another. "Carol and I are so proud of Evan and Rick and their choice to serve our country, as scary as it is to watch them go. We hope and pray they come back to us safe and sound...and that they don't cause too much trouble while deployed."

Everyone chuckled at the light jab. Janet's dad raised his red plastic cup and invited everyone to join him as he gave the boys a cheer. By the time he was finished, and the crowd began chattering and spreading back out again, Janet was standing right beside Rick.

"Hey!" she exclaimed, catching his attention. "Can I talk to you for a sec?"

He looked mildly surprised but then gave her a little smirk and nodded. "Sure."

"Somewhere private," she clarified.

He looked hesitant, but slowly said, "All right. Lead the way."

Falling Again

Turning, Janet led him toward the grove of trees lining the east side of the yard. They made their way into the thicket, moving along a familiar path until they reached a small clearing with a tree house high above them. Christmas lights were strung up along the treehouse's roof and a painted sign that read *Janet's Place* hung next to the ladder leading up the tree.

This was Janet's safe spot. Her own personal hideaway that she still came to when she needed to be alone and escape her fifteen-year-old stresses. It was the perfect place to tell Rick how she felt about him.

She stopped near the ladder and spun around to face him. He stopped, his expression cautious.

"So, what's up Janet?" he asked, sliding his hands into the pockets of his dark jeans. "What'd you want to talk about?"

Janet took a deep breath, fortifying her courage, before saying, "Rick, there's something I want to tell you...before you go overseas, I mean. Not that I don't think you'll come back, but you know...if I don't say, I know I'm going to regret it forever."

She was rambling. She was nervous, and she was making a fool of herself and blowing the one chance she had to do this.

She sucked in another breath and forced herself to calm down before continuing. Rick watched her the whole time, his brow furrowed in confusion. He didn't say anything, though, letting her get her thoughts sorted out.

At last, she managed to spit out, "I love you, Rick. I've loved you for a long time and I couldn't let you leave without you knowing. I want to be with you, Rick."

He stared at her, clearly shocked by her confession.

Janet watched him, her heart racing, and her stomach twisting with anticipation.

Rick swallowed and scratched the back of his neck.

"Um...Janet, that's really flattering, but I don't think it'd be a good idea for us to be together. I mean, you're my best friend's sister, and I'm way too old for you."

Janet shook her head. "That's not true! You're only four years older, and I know you don't want to upset Evan, but he'd get used to it in time..."

"Janet, I'm sorry. I just don't feel that way about you."

Panic seized her. No, no, no, this wasn't how it was supposed to happen. This wasn't how she'd imagined it. He had to feel the same way. He had to! She recalled all the little moments they'd shared throughout the years. All the secret smiles and little winks he'd shot her way. The inside jokes and teasing. It all had to mean something!

Desperation had her acting without thinking. She grabbed hold of the front of his shirt and pushed up onto her toes. She captured his lips with hers and kissed him, pouring all of her feelings for him into that single point of contact.

He had to know how much she really loved him.

It wasn't just a schoolgirl crush. It was real, and it was deep.

Rick didn't respond to her kiss for several moments, and she couldn't tell if he was simply shocked or confused. At length, though, he grabbed her upper arms and pushed her away, breaking the kiss with a scowl.

"Janet!" he barked. "That's enough. You can't just kiss someone without warning."

"I'm sorry!" she exclaimed. "But I needed you to know that this is real! I needed you to feel it!"

Falling Again

"I don't feel it," he snapped, giving her a firm shake. "Do you hear me? Janet, I don't feel that way about you."

"I don't believe you," she insisted. Her heart couldn't take it. "Rick, please, it's me..."

"Janet, enough," he growled. "You don't know what you're talking about. You're only fifteen. You're just a kid with a silly crush. It's not love. You can't know what that's like yet. You don't love me, and I don't love you."

Janet stared up at him, shocked. She didn't want to believe him, but how could he be so cruel to her? He wasn't acting like the Rick she knew. The one she'd grown up with.

She didn't know the man standing in front of her, glaring down at her like she was a nuisance. An annoyance.

A pest.

She shook her head, taking a step back.

"No, stop it," she whimpered. "Stop being so mean..."

"Stop acting like a baby," he replied with a hiss. "Someday, when you're older, you'll realize this isn't what you think, and you'll thank me for this. It might seem harsh now, but I'm being blunt, so you don't get confused. This is for you, Janet."

Tears gathered in the corners of her eyes and began to spill down her cheeks.

"This isn't for me!" she shouted. "You're a coward, Rick! And a bully! I hate you. I hate you!"

At that moment, she did. She hated him as much as she loved him. The emotions were two sides of the same coin: intense, all-consuming, and soul-deep.

Before he could say anything else to her, she turned and ran away from him, heading deeper into the woods.

"Janet!" he shouted after her, but she didn't pause or go back. She couldn't face him after such a humiliating rejection.

She'd been such an idiot. What had she been thinking, telling him how she felt? And then, for him to call her feelings silly...

As Janet weaved through the trees, running as fast as she could, she swore to herself she'd never let this happen to her again. She'd never let someone make her feel the way Rick just had. She'd forget all about her feelings for him and never give her heart to someone who'd throw it away as easily as he had.

* * *

She woke with a start, her heart racing as though she'd really been running through the woods just seconds before.

Janet sat up and looked around. She was in her bed, in her room. Not standing beneath the old treehouse at her childhood home. Why was she dreaming of that night all of a sudden? It'd been ten years since she'd made the mistake of confessing her feelings to Rick Masters. She'd done her best not to think about him much since then, not that it was hard to do so. After he and Evan were honorably discharged from the Navy Seals, Rick had busied himself building up some sort of security business. He hardly ever came home.

She hadn't actually seen him in about three, no, four years, and she didn't have any plans on seeing him any time soon.

So why now?

Why was she dreaming of that night now?

Releasing a sigh, she looked over at her alarm clock. It was two in the morning. She groaned, dropping back down onto her pillows. She had to be up and to the bakery in two hours. Evan would be coming by her house to go with her, and if she wasn't up and ready in time, he'd turn into a relentless nag.

Mumbling under her breath, she curled onto her side, tugging her covers tighter around her and willed herself to go back to sleep and put all thoughts of Rick Masters from her mind.

Chapter 2

Janet

"Janet, I'm serious. This is getting way out of hand. You need security before something bad happens."

Rolling her eyes, Janet glanced toward Evan as they made their way down the sidewalk together, heading in the direction of her bakery. It was so early in the morning that the sun wasn't up yet. Everything was quiet and still, the picturesque downtown of their small town of Mountain Falls, Colorado, still asleep for the most part. There were lights on in a few other stores as their owners prepared for the day ahead.

Usually, Janet was the first one to arrive at her bakery each morning to get started on the donuts and pastries that were most popular at the beginning of the day, and she was typically alone. However, for the past few weeks, Evan had insisted on going with her. He did not like her being alone, given the new, imposing presence that had forced its way into their otherwise quiet and peaceful town.

Though she thought he was being overly protective, there was a part of her that thought he had a point. She wasn't going to admit it out loud, though. He'd go from hovering to straight-up smothering.

"Evan, please," she sighed. "I'm a big girl. I can handle this on my own."

As they reached the front of her shop, they both froze. Janet gritted her teeth as anger burned through her. The door to her bakery was completely covered in flyers for Carlisle Development, a development company trying to get a foothold in town.

A development company desperate to buy her property and run her out of her shop. She'd told them no over and over, but they'd been getting more aggressive until they were all but harassing her.

With a growl, Evan reached out and grabbed at the flyers, ripping a bunch of them from the door.

"This is what I'm talking about!" he exclaimed. "They can't keep doing stuff like this, Janet. This is only going to keep escalating."

Janet moved past him to unlock the front door and walk inside the store. Evan followed, the flyers crumpled in his fist.

"It's just some flyers," she shrugged, not wanting to make a big deal about the situation. Deep down, though, she couldn't completely squash her anxiety. Carlisle Development was proving to be a bigger problem than she'd thought it'd be. Since they'd come rolling into town, wanting to build this large shopping center in the downtown area, they'd been putting pressure on local businesses to sell their properties. Some owners had sold, but there were plenty who refused, including Janet. After saying no, she'd thought that'd be the end of it.

But it hadn't been.

Not by a long shot.

"It's not just flyers," Evan insisted, following her as she made her way to the back of the store and into the kitchen. "You've had those relentless phone calls and that vandalism in the alleyway out back."

"We don't know for sure that was them," Janet pointed out, though she was pretty confident it had been Carlisle Development's people who had spray-painted profanities all over the brick wall behind her store.

Evan snorted. "Yeah, right. You know damn well it was them. You can't underestimate these kinds of people, Janet. They'll do whatever they can to get what they want."

"Evan, I appreciate your concern, but they're just being bullies. Eventually, they'll give up and move on."

"Janet..."

The ring of the front door's bell interrupted Evan and they both turned to the kitchen door with a frown.

"Who could that be?" Evan asked.

"I'd guess Cassie," Janet replied, referring to one of her employees who helped her open the store in the morning. "I don't know why she'd come through the front door, though, and not the back like usual."

She had a bad feeling, and some voice inside her head was telling her it wasn't Cassie or any of her other employees arriving. After sharing a glance with her brother, Janet made her way back out to the storefront.

"Cassie? Is that you..." Her words died on her lips when she spotted the man standing in the middle of her store. Scowling, she hissed, "Harold...what do you want?"

Harold George, representative of Carlisle Development, gave her a smarmy grin. He was tall and slim. He always wore expensive suits and had his blonde hair slicked back so it appeared as oily and slippery as he was.

"Good morning, Janet," he sneered. Then, glancing

Falling Again

beside her, added, "Ah, Evan. A pleasure to see you again as well."

Evan came to a stop next to Janet and growled, "You're not welcome here. Get out."

Harold gave him a condescending wink before saying, "Don't worry. I'm not staying long. I just want to talk to your lovely sister for a moment."

"You're not talking to her alone," Evan snapped. "You're not going to get anywhere near her by yourself from now on."

Harold held up his hands, feigning innocence.

"I don't know what you're talking about, Evan," he said with an arrogant grin. "I just wanted to stop by and bring Janet our latest offer."

He pulled a paper from the inside of his suit jacket and held it out to Janet. Sighing, she took it from him and glanced down at the numbers written on it. It was a hefty sum...six figures. Honestly, more than the property was really worth.

Turning her gaze back up to Harold, she stared right into his eyes as she crumpled up the paper and threw it over her shoulder. Harold's smile remained, but his eyes narrowed and flashed with obvious anger.

"I see," he murmured. "Not happy with that number? I'm not sure we're willing to go any higher, but I can always check..."

"You know I'm just going to say no to that one too," Janet snapped. "It doesn't matter what number you bring me...I'm not selling."

Harold chuckled and shook his head. "You're a stubborn one, Janet. I'll give you that, but it's a thin line between stubbornness and stupid. This offer is more than generous. All our offers have been more than generous. We both know this place isn't worth that much. Anyone else would take this money and run."

Janet folded her arms and arched a brow. "Well, I'm not like anyone else. This is my shop. This is my town. I've worked hard to get where I am and I'm not going to sell out the dream I've put so much time and effort into. So please, just stop this. I don't want your money, and I don't want you to turn this town into another cookie-cutter stop and go for tourists who don't appreciate the people that live here and the lives they've built. So, take your money and shove it."

Harold's smile slipped at that. He gnashed his teeth and his cheeks burned red.

"You're going to regret this, Janet," he hissed. "You don't just dismiss a company like Carlisle Development without facing consequences."

Before Janet could say anything in response, Evan stepped forward and got in Harold's face.

"Did you just threaten my sister?" he growled.

Harold snarled up at him. "It's not a threat...more like a warning. I'd suggest that both of you heed it."

Janet could see that Evan was seconds away from unleashing a world of violence on Harold, so she quickly stepped between the two and pushed them apart.

"That's enough!" she exclaimed. "Harold, get out of my shop! Don't come back, or I'll call the cops. I swear."

Harold looked like he wanted to snap her in half, but he stopped and moved back, giving her room before he made his way to the front of the store. At the door, he shot Janet and Evan a final cold look before storming out.

When he was gone, Janet released a long breath and turned to Evan. He was glaring after Harold, clearly furious. Janet put a hand on his shoulder, drawing his attention back to her.

"Hey," she said with a gentle smile. "It's okay. He's not going to do anything..."

"You don't know that," Evan barked. "You need security, and you're not going to argue with me about it. Mom and Dad think so too, so don't go whining to them hoping they'll be on your side."

Janet sighed and rolled her eyes. "Evan, come on. You're being paranoid."

He ignored her and pulled his phone from his back pocket.

As he began to pull up his contacts, Janet demanded to know, "Who are you calling? Evan? Evan, stop ignoring me!"

"I'm calling Rick," he said as he hit the call button and put the phone to his ear.

Janet froze, her heart racing as her anxiety spiked.

"Rick?" she murmured. "You...you're calling Rick? No, no, no, that's not necessary. You don't need to do that. You don't need to call him..."

Too late, Evan held up a finger to her as he said, "Hey, Rick. How are you doing, man? Good. Look, I have a favor to ask you..."

Clenching her hands into fists, Janet turned and stormed back into the kitchen. She collected the ingredients to make a fresh batch of donuts and started mixing the dough together, hoping she could push Rick from her mind. She hadn't seen him in a while. She couldn't remember how long exactly, but a couple of years. He and Evan were still best friends, but she did her best to avoid any gatherings or social events that he might have been present at.

Since that night when she'd confessed her feelings for him, she'd worked hard to put her broken heart back together and heal her bruised ego. She'd thrown everything into school and then into getting her culinary degree. After that, her focus was on opening the bakery and building her business.

Janet had made sure she hadn't had time to think about Rick Masters for the last ten years. She'd also made sure she'd had no time to give to dating and relationships. She'd never wanted to feel the way Rick had made her feel that night.

If he was her security, though, she wouldn't have much of a choice but to hang around him.

"No, no, that might not be true," she murmured as she began to knead the dough. "He's got a whole firm. A whole team of people working for him. It wouldn't have to be him."

She clung to that thought, desperate for any relief from her growing anxiety.

"Woah, hey, you, okay?" Evan's voice suddenly broke through her thoughts, startling her.

Janet realized she wasn't just kneading her dough but slamming her fists into it and flattening it.

"Dang," she murmured, pushing the ruined dough to the side and turning to face Evan. She released a long breath and met his gaze. "I'm fine. What did Rick say?"

"He's going to meet with us tomorrow," Evan replied with a frown. "Are you really okay?"

"Yes," she insisted, annoyed. "I told you already. Suddenly you care how I feel?"

Evan's eyes widened. "Hey, hold up a second. Why are you attacking me?"

Janet closed her eyes and took a moment to get her temper under control.

"I'm sorry," she muttered. "I am, really. It's not you. I know you're just trying to help. I'm just...stressed."

He gave her a sympathetic look. "I know, but you don't have to worry. Rick and I'll take care of it, yeah? You won't have to worry about Harold or Carlisle Development anymore."

Evan crossed the room toward her and wrapped his arms around her in a tight hug. Janet hugged him back, but she was still irritated with him and not at all happy that he was being so high handed in bringing Rick in. She wouldn't argue with him, though. She'd let him have his way so he'd feel better and give her some breathing room.

Now she just had to figure out what she was going to do about Rick.

Chapter 3

Rick

Pulling into the driveway, he looked up at Evan's imposing two-story Victorian house, impressed. Apparently, contracting was treating his friend very well. Rick parked and climbed out of his truck, gazing around at the neatly trimmed lawn and hedges.

"He has to have a lawn care guy," he said with a grin. No way Evan would keep up such a meticulous-looking property on his own.

Driving through town to get to Evan's had been a bit strange. Rick hadn't been home in a couple of years. Not since his security business had really taken off. He'd been too busy with work to make the time, but when Evan had called asking for his help, Rick hadn't hesitated to say yes. Especially when Evan said the job was protecting Janet.

It'd been so long since he'd seen her, but he still felt protective of the little girl he'd once known. She'd always been like a younger sister to him, and he didn't want to see anything happen to her.

Reaching the front door of the house, Rick knocked

Falling Again

without hesitation. It only took a couple of moments for the door to be opened.

"Hey, man!" Evan exclaimed, reaching out a hand for Rick to shake. "Thanks for coming on such short notice. Come on in. Janet's waiting in the living room."

Rick shook his friend's hand and then followed Evan into the house. The foyer was well decorated with a high ceiling and vases of flowers perched on entryway tables.

"Did you have a decorator?" Rick asked with a smirk.

Evan chuckled. "Not exactly. Janet's taken it upon herself to make sure the house isn't a bare-bones bachelor pad. I learned a long time ago just to let her have her way. It's a lot easier that way."

Rick remembered how stubborn Janet could be. She'd always gotten her way. She'd been a little spoiled, but it hadn't made her a brat. On the contrary, she'd been a pretty sweet kid. She'd had her brother and parents wrapped around her little finger, and if Rick was honest, he was too.

He was actually a little excited to see her again.

They entered the living room and Rick spotted a figure sitting on a couch by a large stone fireplace.

"Janet, come say hi to Rick," Evan said, catching the person's attention.

Rick froze as the woman rose to her feet and faced them. It took him a moment to recognize Janet. She was no longer the little girl he'd once known. She'd grown up...and she was gorgeous.

She wasn't much taller than she'd been as a teenager, but she was soft and curvy in all the right places. Her long brown hair was pulled back into an elegant ponytail, and her bright green eyes flashed when her gaze met his.

For a moment, he was completely dumbstruck. He

wasn't certain what he'd been expecting walking through that door, but it hadn't been this. It hadn't been *her.*

Jeez...this may be a trickier job than I thought.

Janet came to a stop in front of him. She looked him up and down with an arched brow and a frown. She didn't look at all happy to see him, truth be told.

Her reaction to seeing him caught him off guard.

"Hey, Janet," he said with a cautious grin. "It's been a while."

She shrugged. "I guess."

What the heck? What was going on? Why was she giving him the cold-shoulder?

Evan looked between the two of them, seemingly as confused by the interaction as Rick was.

"Um...should we sit and talk?" he suggested in an uncertain tone.

"Works for me," Janet sighed, turning to walk back to the couch. She plopped back down on the cushions and waited for Rick and Evan to join her. The two exchanged confused looks before going to sit with her.

"Okay," Evan began, clapping his hands together. "So, here's the deal. There's this development company that's trying to bully Janet out of her bakery. She's told them no countless times, but they just don't quit and they're escalating their efforts."

"What's that mean?" Rick asked, glancing toward Janet. She wouldn't look at him, though.

Evan answered instead. "There's been some vandalism. We can't prove that it was them, but we know it was. They've covered the front door with flyers promoting their development, and yesterday, their representative, Harold George, came into the bakery and threatened Janet."

That got Rick's guard up. "What did he say exactly?"

Falling Again

Finally, Janet was the one to speak. "He said I'd be sorry. That there'd be consequences for turning them down."

She spoke softly, almost in a monotone, but Rick could sense the smallest quiver of fear in her voice. She might try to shrug off the threat this company posed, but a part of her was legitimately afraid of them.

Rick didn't like that. He didn't like that one bit.

The thought of her frightened at all made him clench his teeth.

"How many people work in the bakery during the day?" he asked.

Janet didn't answer, so Evan sighed and said, "Apart from Janet, Cassie, Maria, and Annie work in the morning. Then, in the afternoon, she has a guy named Billy and another girl, Jasmine, who tend to work in the front of the store."

"All right," Rick nodded, keeping his tone as even and steady as he could. "So, what are you thinking security-wise? Cameras? Alarms?"

Evan nodded. "Yes, all of it. Plus, I want Janet to have a personal bodyguard for the time being as well."

"What?" Janet exclaimed, turning her gaze up to her brother. "What are you talking about? I don't need a bodyguard, Evan. That's too far..."

"I'm not arguing about this, Janet," Evan snapped. "Until we figure out what to do about Carlisle Development, I want you to have protection. I don't want Harold to get the chance to corner you alone. Got it?"

Rick watched Janet's reaction. He could see her frustration in her expression and in the way she clenched her jaw. He could see she wanted to argue the point further, but Rick knew how stubborn Evan was. How controlling he could be. Not in a bad way...just in a firm way.

Janet released a long breath and relaxed into her seat, crossing her arms over her chest like a petulant child. She made no further argument, though.

"When can you get a guy up here?" Evan asked, leaning forward and resting his elbows on his knees.

Rick looked between Janet and Evan and answered, "Right away. I'll be stepping in as Janet's bodyguard."

"What?" Evan and Janet exclaimed together. While Evan appeared surprised, Janet looked totally horrified. Rick frowned at her, confused, but she blinked at him and jerked her gaze away.

"Aren't you too busy for this?" Evan asked, pulling Rick's focus back to him. "I mean, don't get me wrong, we appreciate the thought, but we don't expect you to take it on yourself."

Rick shook his head. "No, I'm not too busy. Not for this. I'm personally going to ensure Janet's safety. You guys are like family. I only use my best people for my family."

"So, you're saying you're the best?" Janet scoffed, her eyes still firmly focused away from him.

"Yeah, I am," he said without hesitation. He didn't care if she thought he was arrogant. Plenty of people did, but it wasn't arrogance if what he said was true. He was the best. He'd built his security firm using his own skills and abilities. Even though he didn't really go out on the jobs himself anymore, that didn't mean he'd gone soft. His time as a Navy Seal had taught him to always stay sharp and ready. He continued to abide by that mindset, even as a civilian.

Janet rolled her eyes. "Good to know your ego is still intact."

"Janet, knock it off," Evan hissed.

Falling Again

Rick shot his friend a smile and shook his head. "It's all right. She's entitled to question my ability to keep her safe. It's her prerogative."

"Yeah, but she doesn't need to insult you," Evan huffed, glaring at his sister.

Rick didn't understand the tension rolling off Janet, but he didn't want to cause any sort of conflict between the siblings.

"Really, it's okay," Rick insisted. "This is a stressful situation. I get it and I don't take anything personally. Now, let's talk about schematics..."

They spent the next half hour going over the details of the bakery's security, as well as the contract. Rick refused to charge them a penny for his services, despite Evan's protests. It was really only Evan and Rick talking, as Janet remained stone-cold and silent. Despite what he'd said about understanding how stressful the situation was, he really couldn't understand why she was being so cool toward him. It bothered him, and while he kept things professional during the meeting, he grew increasingly determined to figure out what was going on with her.

"All right, then we've got everything figured out," Evan said with a satisfied nod once they worked out all the details. Rick and Evan shook hands as they all stood. He turned to Janet and asked, "Everything sounds good to you?"

She shrugged and sighed. "Yeah, fine. It all sounds fine. I need to get going."

"Janet!" Evan exclaimed, baffled, as she hurried out of the room.

Rick patted Evan's shoulder and assured him, "Don't worry. I've had a few clients who are resistant to protection at first, but they always appreciate it in the end. I'll go talk to her and smooth things over quickly."

Evan released a quick breath. "Yeah, all right. See what you can do. I'm not sure what her deal is."

Rick nodded and then left to go after Janet.

He stepped outside and stood on the front porch as he gazed around for her. Spotting her walking toward her car, Rick jogged after her.

"Janet! Wait," he called.

She stopped, her hand on the car door handle. As he drew close to her, he could sense that tension radiating off her again. When he reached her, she slowly turned around and glared up at him.

"What is it?" she asked in a cool tone.

Rick arched a brow, baffled by her attitude. "Look, I know this is a lot to take in, but I promise, I'm going to make sure your life isn't overly disturbed."

"Great," she murmured. "Is that all?"

He frowned and shook his head. "What's the matter with you? Did I do something? I don't understand why you're acting like this."

She blinked up at him, looking shocked.

"Are you serious right now?" she asked. "Don't act like you don't know what you did."

He shook his head. "I don't. Tell me what's going on, Janet. This whole thing will be a lot easier if we clear the air of whatever is bothering you."

She stared at him, clearly stunned. Slowly, she shook her head and let out a humorless bark of laughter.

"Oh, my God. Of course, you don't remember! I shouldn't be surprised, you arrogant jerk."

"Woah!" Rick exclaimed. "Hold on! I'm sorry I don't

remember, but it's been years since we've even seen each other..."

Janet rolled her eyes and growled, "Yeah, well, I suppose you wouldn't remember. It wasn't the first time your heart was broken, after all."

Rick blinked. "What are you talking about?"

Sighing, her shoulders slumped forward in defeat, and she finally explained, "The night before you and Evan were first deployed, I pulled you aside and told you...I told you I loved you, and you completely rejected me. You called my feelings silly and said I was too young to really understand what I was saying. I was humiliated and heartbroken. Do you remember that now?"

Rick furrowed his brow as he tried to think back and remember what she was talking about. Slowly, the memories of that night filtered into his mind, and he could suddenly see Janet's young face staring up at him, her bright gaze shimmering with hurt.

"Oh," he murmured, scratching the back of his head, his gut twisting with guilt. "I remember now. Sorry...I'd forgotten all about that night."

Her face turned bright red, and her eyes darkened with rage.

"Right," she hissed. "Again, why am I surprised?"

Whirling away from him, she opened her car door and slid into the front seat. Before she could shut the door again, Rick grabbed it and held it open.

"Janet, hold on," he growled. "Let's talk about this. I want us to be comfortable around each other. It'll make this process so much easier."

"Let go of my door, Rick," she demanded in an ice-cold voice.

Rick hesitated a moment before he let go of the door

and stepped back so she could slam it shut. He watched as she started the car and sped away down the driveway.

With a sigh, he shook his head and ran an agitated hand through his hair.

This job just got way more complicated than he'd anticipated.

Chapter 4

Janet

"So, wait...you're going to have a bodyguard now?"

"More like a glorified babysitter," Janet growled as she drove through town. "And it's Evan's friend, Rick, so it's not like I can really refuse. But, Cassie, I swear to God, he's the last person I want hovering around me day in and day out."

Cassie, who was not only an employee but a genuine friend, sighed, the sound reverberating through the car. When Janet had stormed out of Evan's house, she'd gotten in her car and immediately called Cassie, needing to vent to someone who had no connection to Rick Masters.

"I mean, maybe it won't be so bad," Cassie said at length. "The way things are going with Carlisle, there might be some benefit to having an ex-Navy Seal hovering nearby."

Janet scoffed. "You're only saying that because you've never met him. Trust me, having Rick Masters lurking around will not be a good thing."

"I'm sorry, Janet," Cassie replied. "I just hope all this

blows over soon. I can't stand all this stress, never knowing what Carlisle will do next."

"Yeah, totally agree," Janet murmured.

There was a short pause before Cassie asked, "Hey, Janet, where are you going?"

"Nowhere," Janet murmured, her cheeks flushing.

"Janet! Are you going to the bakery? You need to go home and get some sleep!"

"I'm fine," Janet said dismissively. "I just need to blow off some steam."

"Angry baking is not the answer. You waste more dough than you actually make."

"That's not true." It might have been true. "Anyway, I'm almost there. I'll see you in the morning, Cassie. Goodnight!"

"Goodnight, Janet," Cassie grumbled.

Janet ended the call and released a long breath. She didn't want to go home. She'd have nothing to do there but sit and stew about Rick and how much of a jerk he was. Instead, she'd decided to go from Evan's house to the bakery to angry-bake, just like Cassie had guessed. It was one of her go-to activities for stress release, and she had so much anger and frustration boiling within her, she figured she'd be baking for the rest of the night.

She couldn't believe it. Couldn't believe the audacity of that man. One of the most significant moments of her life had been barely a blip in his memory. Crushing her heart had been absolutely no big deal to him. That moment had changed her life and her perspective of the world, and it wasn't even worth a place in his memory.

Tears stung the corners of her eyes, but she blinked and fought not to let them fall. She refused to shed any more tears because of that man.

Falling Again

Janet was angrily punching at dough when she heard the front door open. She'd been in such a rush to get to the kitchen, she'd forgotten to lock it. Tensing, she turned and eased her way out of the kitchen, her stomach twisting with anxiety.

"Hello?" she called. "Who's there? We're not open!"

"Which is why you shouldn't leave the front door unlocked." Rick walked into view with an exasperated expression.

Janet gasped and jumped. Placing a hand over her heart, she declared, "What are you doing here? You scared the life out of me!"

He came to stop in front of her and she had to tilt her head back to meet his gaze.

"You and I need to talk, Janet," he told her with a frown. "I'm not going to be able to properly protect you if we can't put this mess behind us."

Janet clenched her teeth and glared up at him.

"You know, dismissing my first heartbreak as 'this mess,' really isn't a good start to this conversation," she growled.

He released a long sigh. "Okay, that's not how I meant it. Come on, Janet. It was ten years ago..."

"You're right, it was ten years ago, and it still hurts! That should tell you something."

She spun away from him and stormed back into the kitchen. She heard his exasperated growl before he started following her.

"All right, I get it, I'm sorry, okay? But let's be honest, Janet, you were just a kid back then. Hell, I was still just a kid. Neither of us really knew what love actually was."

"Well, you certainly set yourself up as the authority on the subject," she hissed. "You made me feel like an idiot, Rick. Like I was so small and insignificant, I could just disappear, and it wouldn't matter to you. Do you know how much that hurts? Do you know how hard I had to work to build my self-confidence back up after that?"

She stopped and turned to face him again, wanting to see his reaction. He flinched and swallowed, with his Adam's apple bobbing.

"I tried to turn you down gently," he said at length, his tone soft. "You just wouldn't listen. You were so convinced I felt something for you that you wouldn't let it go. I had no choice but to be cruel."

Janet's heart twisted in her chest. He wasn't wrong. She could admit that much. Still, that didn't take the bite out of his condescending words. Didn't make his rejection any more palatable..

"You're right," she murmured. "I was just a kid, and maybe it was just a stupid crush, but apart from Evan, you were the one person in the world who I never thought would hurt me...and you did, Rick. You hurt me so badly I can't even look at you without my stomach roiling."

"Janet, come on," he pleaded. "You're not being fair."

She shrugged. "Love's not fair, Rick. I'm just following its rules."

"There has to be some way we can move past this," Rick said, sounding almost exhausted. "What can I do to fix things between us?"

Janet gazed at him for several moments, feeling helpless as she shrugged and shook her head.

"I...I honestly don't know," she whispered. "I'm just not sure I can risk you hurting me again."

His expression shifted into one of desperation. "Come on, Janet, please. There has to be something..."

A sudden crash startled them both. Before Janet could fully comprehend what was happening, Rick dove for her,

Falling Again

covering her head with his hand and pushing her to the floor. He shielded her body with his, and it was only at that moment that she fully realized how big he was...and how instantly safe she felt in his arms.

When there was no further commotion, Rick slowly released Janet and stood up.

"What was that?" she breathed, her voice trembling.

He shook his head but didn't speak as he moved toward the doorway. He waved his hand at her, clearly wanting her to stay put, but like hell she was going to do that. She stood and crept after him. He shot her an annoyed look but didn't argue with her. Stepping in front of her, he led her out to the front of the store. They gazed around, not immediately seeing anything in the dark storefront, but when Janet's gaze landed on the front display window, she gasped.

It was broken. She hurried to turn the light on, ignoring Rick's grunt of disapproval. Broken glass was scattered across the wood floor of the bakery. Fury welled up within her as she gazed around, looking for whatever it was that had shattered her window.

"Here," Rick said, bending down to pick something up off the floor. "They must have thrown this."

Janet hurried toward him. He held out a brick. She reached for it, but he snatched it back.

"No," he shook his head.

She frowned as he tried to hold the brick in such a way that she couldn't really see it.

"What?" she snapped. "Rick, what is it? Show me!"

She glared at him, determined to wrestle the brick from his hand if need be. After several moments, he sighed in defeat and held the brick out for her to take.

Janet grabbed it and looked it over. There was a message written on it in white paint.

Get out. No more chances.

Stunned, she stared at the angry-looking letters for several seconds as her body went numb. Her fingers went limp, and the brick dropped from her grasp to the floor below. Her fury quickly turned to fear. This was too much. Too far. She knew deep down that it wasn't an idle threat.

She was in real danger.

Janet's knees suddenly gave out and she would have fallen to the floor just like the brick, but Rick caught her. He wrapped his arms around her and picked her up, cradling her against his broad chest. Without a word, he carried her back into the kitchen. Setting her down on a stool, he leaned down, so they were eye level as he held her face in his hands. His touch was gentle and soothing, but she could still feel the strength in his fingers.

"You're okay," he told her in a soft but firm voice. "Everything's going to be okay."

His tenderness and care broke her. All the stress and anxiety she'd been holding onto the past couple of months came bubbling to the surface and burst free. Janet's eyes filled with tears and spilled down her cheeks as she let out a shaky sob. Without thinking, she reached for him, wrapping her arms around him and hugging him as tightly as she could. He returned her embrace, holding her and rubbing her back as she cried into his chest.

"I swear I'm going to take care of this for you," he promised her in a low, hard tone. "Whatever it takes, I'm going to make sure that no one threatens you ever again. I'll protect you, Janet. I promise."

At that moment, Janet didn't care about their past, or the fact that he'd hurt her. She didn't care about how awkward it was going to be to have him around, or how angry she still was with him.

Falling Again

At that moment, all that mattered was that he was there. He was an anchor in the storm, and she clung to him for dear life. Wrapped around him, she felt safe. She felt cared for, and that was what she needed.

Whatever happened between them in the morning didn't matter to her as she sat crying and soaking up the comfort he offered her. For that night, all that mattered was that he was there, and she wasn't alone.

Chapter 5

Rick

He had never felt such intense dueling emotions before. On the one hand, he was enraged. If the person who'd thrown that brick were standing in front of him at that moment, he couldn't be certain he wouldn't beat them to a bloody pulp. He was seething, a primal need to deal out retribution burning through him.

However, he was also worried for Janet. He felt a strong sense of protectiveness over her that went beyond anything he'd felt for a regular client before. As he'd held her while she'd cried, he'd been desperate to make her feel better. To make her feel safe. Watching her distress had been like a punch in the gut, stealing the wind from him and breaking his heart in two.

Janet was strong and stubborn, but a person could only take so much before they cracked. She'd looked as if the weight of the world was crashing down onto her shoulders, and all Rick wanted to do was bear that weight for her.

After she'd calmed down, he'd insisted on taking her home himself. She hadn't argued, likely still too scared and exhausted to put up a fight with him. She was quiet the

Falling Again

whole ride over to her house, leaning her head against the window and staring up at the night sky with an unreadable expression on her face.

Arriving at her place, Rick quickly took stock of the property. It was nice. A quaint little one-story with a yard as neat and well-kept as her brother's. He didn't question if she had a hand in caring for the place like he had Evan. Rick knew Janet would work hard to keep her home looking cozy and clean.

He followed her inside, and again, she didn't protest. She led him into her living room and sat on the floral-patterned couch. When he sat next to her, she didn't react. She wrapped her arms around her torso and rested her elbows on her knees as she stared blankly at the floor.

"Janet," he gently said, reaching over to put a hand on her shoulder. "I know you're really shaken up right now, but I need you to help me understand exactly what we're dealing with here."

"We already told you everything," she murmured, not looking up at him.

He shook his head. "No, Evan told me everything. I want to hear from you. I want your perspective on everything because you are the one I'm protecting. I want to know what it is you're scared of happening next."

She didn't reply for several long moments, and Rick didn't push her. He kept his hand on her shoulder, though, hoping the physical connection between them made her feel more secure and safe.

Finally, she released a breath and looked up at him.

"It started innocently enough," she began. "Carlisle Development began sending representatives into the area to talk to business owners. At first, they only said they were scouting the area for potential building sites, but then their story quickly changed, and they wanted to buy us all out and build on our properties instead. Harold came to me with an offer, and I turned it down. I wasn't interested in the money, and I don't want to see our town overrun by big companies that don't really care about the community. I thought that would be it, especially when I heard I wasn't the only one who didn't sell. I figured Carlisle Development would readjust their plans or simply move onto another town. I was wrong."

"They kept coming," Rick said.

She nodded. "Yeah. Harold started coming to the bakery once every week, then once every three days, then every other day, and then nearly every day. He didn't always talk to me or bring up selling to Carlisle. Some days he'd just wander the shop, interacting with other customers, and lingering as though he were going to buy something. He rarely did, though, He was just always there."

"He wanted to make his presence known," Rick sighed.

"Exactly. The threat was silent, but it was obvious."

"It's a pretty common scare tactic," he said. "I've seen it before."

"Well, he didn't stop there," Janet continued. "We started getting phone calls throughout the day. No one would talk when we answered, but they kept our phone line busy so people had a hard time calling in orders. The alleyway behind the store started getting tagged with all sorts of images and messages meant to scare us. No matter how often I had the walls cleaned back there, there'd always be new graffiti by the end of the week. It was annoying, but at least the customers didn't see it. It worried my employees, though."

"How much do they know about the situation?"

"They all know Carlisle hasn't let up trying to buy the

Falling Again

place," she explained. "Only Cassie knows all the details. She's my right hand and I wanted her to be aware in case something happened when I wasn't there."

"Smart," Rick nodded. "I'm going to want to talk to her, if that's all right?"

"Yeah, it's fine," she murmured, shrugging her shoulders. "I suppose I'll have to introduce you to everyone. They're going to be curious about the random guy following me around everywhere."

Rick chuckled and rubbed his cheek. "I promise I'll be discreet, Janet. I'll be close enough to make sure you're safe, but far enough away that you won't feel smothered."

She glanced up at him and regarded him a moment before saying, "Thanks. I think I can live with that."

"Good," he nodded. "I want you to trust me, Janet. I'm going to look into Carlisle Development and see if I can find something to drive them out of town. I won't rest until you're safe and your business is secure. I promise."

She stared at him, her body visibly relaxing as she slowly smiled.

"I'll admit, I wasn't thrilled about this when Evan insisted on hiring you for security, but I do feel better knowing you'll be around. I'm sorry I was so cold earlier. I do appreciate you taking care of me tonight."

He smiled softly. "I'd say it's the job, but it's more than that, Janet. We've known each other forever. I care about your well-being."

"I know," she murmured, her gaze locked with his. "I know that, Rick."

Something seemed to pass between them at that moment. The air seemed to crackle and grow thick with tension, and before he realized what he was doing, Rick leaned in and pressed his lips to hers. Janet returned his kiss, cupping the side of his face as they slowly explored each other. A haze seemed to fall over his mind and he reached up to graze his fingers along her jaw.

When a moan escaped her, though, it snapped Rick back to reality.

He couldn't do this.

Not with Janet.

She was off-limits to him. Not only was she his client, but she was Evan's sister. No matter how much she'd grown and matured, he couldn't let himself forget that.

Rick jerked his lips away from hers and quickly pushed to his feet.

"You must be tired," he muttered, not looking at her and scratching the back of his neck nervously. "I should go and let you sleep. I...I'm sorry. I'll see you tomorrow."

Before she could say a word in response or protest, he turned and hurried out of her house and away from the temptation she presented to him.

Chapter 6

Janet

"Uh, Janet? You okay? Those eclairs look pretty stuffed."

Blinking, Janet looked up from the tray of pastries she'd been filling with cream to find Cassie gazing at her with an arched brow and curious frown. Glancing back down at the éclair in her hand, Janet found the filling was oozing out of one end. Shaking her head, she set the éclair back on the tray and put the pastry bag of cream to the side.

"Phew!" she sighed. "Guess I was spacing out."

"I'd say," Cassie replied, with concern in her green gaze. "You okay? You seem a little off today."

Janet and Cassie stood in the bakery's kitchen, working on fresh batches of donuts and pastries to keep the display cases in the front of the store full. Annie and Maria were out front, taking care of customers as they reached the tail-end of the morning rush. Janet grabbed a towel and wiped her hands before leaning back against the stainless-steel island in the middle of the kitchen. She folded her arms and met Cassie's eyes.

"I'm just stressed over this whole Carlisle Development thing," she said. "They've gotten way more aggressive than I'd have expected. I don't get it. Can't they just take no for an answer?"

Cassie's expression turned sympathetic. She pushed a strand of her curly red hair that had escaped from her ponytail behind her ear.

"Yeah, I can imagine how difficult it's been for you," she nodded. "Those people are like cockroaches. They just keep coming back, no matter how many times you try to squish them."

Janet nodded, agreeing completely. However, she hadn't been entirely honest with Cassie. Yes, Carlisle Development was a constant worry in her head, but it wasn't what she had been lost in thought about.

Her mind had been full of thoughts of Rick and the kiss they'd shared the night before.

It had taken her by complete surprise, but it had felt so natural and right to respond to his lips on hers, she hadn't been able to help herself. Suddenly, she'd been that young girl again, in love with her brother's best friend and certain he felt the same way about her.

However, just as he had back then, he'd broken away from her and bolted.

Why? Why did he keep running away, when it was so obvious there was something between them? Some kind of chemistry that made the air sizzle between them whenever they were close to each other. She curled her fingers around the edge of the island behind her as she recalled what his lips pressed against hers had felt like. The thought warmed her from the inside out. She knew she shouldn't let these feelings overtake her again as he was just as likely to hurt her now as he had all those years ago, standing under her treehouse.

Still, she couldn't push them away, and she couldn't stop wondering if Rick was feeling anything more for her at that moment.

As she was lost in thought, Annie suddenly came running into the kitchen from the front, her blue eyes wide and her cheeks flushed. She was older, in her mid-fifties, and usually didn't startle easily. She looked alarmed at that moment, though, which had Janet instantly on alert.

"Janet!" she exclaimed. "That Harold guy is here again and is demanding to see you. He's upsetting the customers."

Gnashing her teeth, Janet replied, "I'll be right out, Annie. Don't worry."

Nodding, Annie turned and hurried back out to the front of the store. Growling, Janet ripped off her apron and tossed it onto the nearby counter.

"What are you going to do, Janet?" Cassie asked, her eyes wide with worry.

"I'm going to throw him out," Janet hissed. "Then I'm going to file for a restraining order. This nonsense is going to stop."

Before Cassie could reply, Janet stormed out of the kitchen and made her way to the front counter. Annie and Maria, another older woman with black hair and hazel eyes, both looked her way with anxious expressions.

"Ah, there you are," Harold, standing on the opposite side of the counter, said with a smirk. Janet looked around at her customers, who were watching the scene unfold with a mixture of curiosity and anxiety.

Janet turned back to him, her nostrils flared and eyes narrowed into a glare.

"What do you want this time, Harold?" she demanded to know.

"I've just come to talk, Janet," he replied with a condescending chuckle. "To see if you've come to your senses yet."

"I'm not interested, Harold, and you know it," Janet sighed, annoyed. "You can leave now. There's nothing more for us to discuss."

Harold put his elbows on the counter and leaned closer to her.

"There's plenty more for us to discuss," he insisted. "Rising property taxes, bank bonds...you know, things that might make it difficult for a small business with a single owner to stay afloat."

Janet released a hiss of breath. It wasn't the first time he'd made such threats.

"If you don't get out, I'm calling the police," she snapped.

"You're making this more difficult than it needs to be," he told her. "I heard you had an incident last night."

He glanced toward the boarded-up front window and looked back at her with a knowing grin.

Janet gritted her teeth. "Yeah, a bit unfortunate. I'm sure you and your associates wouldn't know anything about that, now would you?"

Harold raised his brows and shrugged. "I'm sure I don't know what you're talking about. I'd hate to think this neighborhood is getting dangerous, though. Next time, it might be more than a window that breaks."

Janet froze, staring at him with a racing heart. The rest of the bakery went quiet as his words sank in.

"Are you threatening me?" she murmured.

Falling Again

He tilted his head and regarded her with that condescending glint in his eye.

"No threats," he chuckled. "Just being a friendly neighbor. Just looking out for you. A single young woman needs to be careful."

The way he looked at her was predatory. It actually frightened her.

She swallowed, unable to think of anything to say in response. He might actually be willing to hurt her.

Suddenly, the front door's bell rang as it was opened. Janet glanced toward the door and felt a wave of relief when she spotted Rick storming toward them. He came up behind Harold and grabbed his shoulder, startling the man.

"Excuse me," Rick growled. "But the owner of this establishment has told you to get out. I suggest you do so before I'm forced to throw you out."

Harold turned with a snarl. "Who are you? Get your hands off me."

Rick gripped Harold's shirt tighter.

"Get out and don't come back," he hissed. "You'll regret it otherwise."

Harold seemed to recognize the threat standing before him. He looked Rick up and down, taking in his large, muscular form, and let out a deep breath.

"Very well," he muttered. "I'll go. For now. But this isn't over." He turned to glare back at Janet. "Watch yourself, Janet. I'll be back."

Rick let him go, but followed him out the front door. Once Harold was gone, Rick came back and marched right toward Janet. He made his way behind the counter and grabbed her hand. He led her back to the kitchen and she didn't resist.

When they reached the kitchen, Rick looked over at Cassie.

"Can you give us a minute?" he asked.

She nodded, her eyes wide with surprise. Turning, Cassie hurried away, leaving Janet and Rick alone.

"Are you all right?" he asked, taking hold of her shoulders and looking her over, as if searching for any injuries.

"I'm fine," she said. "He didn't hurt me or anything. Just threatened me."

He released a long breath, brushing his thumbs over her cheeks before letting her go.

"I don't want you to worry," he told her. "I've got a plan. I just need you to be patient, but I promise, I'm going to take care of this. You won't have to worry about that jerk or Carlisle Development soon enough."

Janet smiled. She believed him. Whatever he had to do, he'd protect her. She was overcome with gratitude, having been so frightened just a moment ago. Stepping closer to him, she wrapped her arms around his waist and hugged him tight.

Rick tensed at first, but then he slowly relaxed and returned her embrace. They stayed like that for a long moment. Janet soaked in his warmth and took comfort in his strength.

Slowly, she raised her face up toward his, and he gazed down at her. She found she couldn't resist his pull, and pushed herself onto her tiptoes to close the distance between them. Her lips met his, and he didn't pull away.

The kiss was tender. A gentle exploration rather than a devouring. Janet didn't want to push Rick too much too fast, because she didn't want him to pull away and run again.

Being like this with him felt too good. Too right. She didn't want the moment to end.

However, it could only last for so long, and Rick seemed to snap out of whatever daze he'd fallen under. He broke the kiss and abruptly stepped away from her.

Janet stared up at him, baffled. Why did he keep doing this?

"I...I'm sorry," he muttered. "I should go."

"Wait!" Janet exclaimed before he could turn and flee from her. She reached out and grabbed his wrist, pulling him to a stop. "Don't go, Rick. Please."

He froze, but he didn't turn back to her. "Janet, please... I'm trying to do the right thing here..."

"Then you need to explain what that is," she insisted. "Why do you keep running away from me? Why do you keep pushing me away?"

He didn't answer right away, and for a moment, she thought he'd just ignore her question and continue on his way.

However, he surprised her by releasing a long breath and slowly turning to her.

He gazed down at her with an expression that seemed heartsick.

"All right," he murmured with a nod. "I'll tell you, but you're not going to like it."

Janet took in a deep breath and put her hands on her hips. "Just tell me, and I'll decide if I like it or not."

Sighing, he ran a hand through his hair, and Janet braced herself for whatever it was he was going to say to her.

Chapter 7

Rick

He didn't want to admit how guilty he felt. He didn't want her to know that he wanted her, but resisted because he was certain he couldn't have her.

Yes, he could admit to himself that he was attracted to Janet. More than that, actually. He was fascinated by her and couldn't get her off his mind. The moment he'd seen her at Evan's house, he'd known he was in trouble. Then, talking with her the night before, seeing how brave and intelligent she was, he'd realized he was a goner.

"Well?" Janet insisted. "Are you going to tell me or not? I think I have a right to know why you keep jerking me around like this, Rick. It's driving me crazy."

Rick released a long breath and nodded. "Yes, yes, I know. You're right. I owe you an explanation. It's just... complicated."

"Then uncomplicate it," she snapped.

He almost chuckled at that. He liked that she didn't put up with other people's baloney. When she wanted something, she didn't just go after it, she demanded it.

He was afraid, though, that once he finished telling her what he needed to, she might end up hating him and wanting nothing to do with him. That thought terrified him, but he knew he didn't have a choice.

"Rick!" Janet exclaimed.

"All right, all right!" he growled. "Just...just promise me you'll hear me out and not bolt or anything like that."

"Kind of a hypocritical request coming from you," she grumbled. "But alright. If that's what it takes to get you to open up, I promise not to bolt."

He grinned and nodded. "I appreciate that." He took another deep breath and steadied himself before admitting, "I remember that night, ten years ago. The night you told me you loved me. I've never forgotten it."

She blinked, clearly stunned. "You...lied?"

He grimaced and nodded. "I did. I'm sorry."

"You made me feel like an idiot when you said you didn't remember," she told him with a baffled shake of her head. "Why? Why did you pretend not to remember?"

Rick rubbed the back of his neck, his heart hammering as he forced the words past his lips.

"Back then, when you told me how you felt about me, I pushed you away because you were my best friend's sister," he explained. "And you were still so young. I really didn't think you knew what you were talking about, and I do apologize for making that assumption. That was ignorant of me."

She frowned, her brow furrowed with obvious confusion.

"Okay, sure, but I don't really understand what you're saying. You pushed me away because I'm Evan's sister...not because you didn't feel anything for me?"

With a sigh, he nodded. "Yes, that's it exactly."

Her eyes widened and she appeared stunned. "So...so you did feel something for me back then?"

Rick took a step toward her and took hold of her hand. "Yes, I did. I've always cared for you, Janet, but I hid my feelings because I didn't think being with you was a line I could cross. I couldn't do that to Evan. He was my best friend and we were going to war together. I didn't want to do anything to betray him, and at the time, I thought that included feeling anything for you."

She stared up at him, in disbelief. He'd clearly shocked her with his confession and he waited for her response, nervous as to what it would be. Anger? Hurt? Disappointment?

He braced himself for whatever it was she had in store for him.

At last, she finally said, "Okay, I can understand that. I still don't like that you said the things you did that night. You really hurt me when you called me a silly kid. My feelings for you were genuine and I was aware enough of myself to understand them."

"I know," he assured her. "Again, I'm so sorry I made you feel that way. I didn't know how to handle the situation, and I handled it badly."

"You could've just told me the truth," she murmured, her gaze pained. "I would've understood. I would've waited for you."

Rick blinked, taken aback by that statement.

"I couldn't have asked that of you," he said. "You needed to live your life while we were enlisted. I'd have hated myself for holding you back."

She narrowed her eyes. "Well, that should have been a decision we made together. You shouldn't have cut me out of it like you did."

Falling Again

He gulped at the sharp tone in her voice. "You're right. I get that now. I was stupid back then. Stupid and short-sighted."

Closing her eyes, Janet released a long breath and shook her head. "Okay, so now what?"

"What do you mean?"

"We're adults now," she stated bluntly. "We can be together if we want. Right?"

Furrowing his brow, he slowly nodded. "Right."

"If Evan has a problem with it, he's also an adult and can get over it."

He chuckled but nodded again. "Yes, I suppose that's right as well."

"So..." She stepped forward so she was pressed against him. "Are we on the same page yet?"

His heart hammering, he moved his hands up her arms, stroking her gently.

"I think we are."

Her lips curled into a relieved smile. "So if I kiss you right now, will you run away again?"

"Why don't you try it and find out?"

Chuckling softly, she slipped her arms around his neck and pulled him down to her. Their lips met in a sweet kiss that turned hungry in a moment. Hunger filled him instead of guilt, and he gripped her waist, pulling her flush against him.

This was the most intense kiss they'd shared yet, and it was because there was nothing holding him back anymore. Janet was right. They were adults. They could choose to be with each other if that's what they wanted.

And it's what he wanted. It's what he'd wanted for years.

Janet Meyers was so entwined into his soul, he didn't

think he'd ever be able to untangle himself from her...not that he had any intention of trying.

Before the kiss went too far and they lost control of themselves right there in the bakery kitchen, Janet pulled her lips from his with a giggle.

Rick smiled down at her.

"Feel the need to flee?" she asked with a wink.

He shook his head, pressing another kiss to her forehead. "Not at all. I'm right where I'm supposed to be."

That appeared to make her melt and she pulled him in for another brief kiss before pushing him away with a breathless laugh.

"Okay, that's enough," she grinned. "You need to get out of here now before you lose control and ravage me on the eclairs."

Laughing softly, he replied, "I'm pretty sure you're the one on the verge of ravaging me. Control yourself, woman. This is a place of business."

She laughed again and started pushing him to the door. He let her move him out of the kitchen, but not before shooting her a wink over his shoulder.

"I'll see you after business hours," he told her in a teasing tone.

Her gaze grew hooded and her eyes flashed with heat. "I'll be waiting."

With that promise hanging between them, Rick left the shop to resume his watchful post out of sight, and put his plan for Carlisle Development into action.

Chapter 8

Janet

"Janet! Janet, you've got to see what's on the news!"

Frowning, Janet looked up from the bread dough she was kneading as Maria came rushing into the kitchen from the front of the bakery.

"What are you talking about?" she asked.

Maria didn't answer right away. She walked straight to the small TV that hung on the wall near the corner opposite of where Janet stood. Janet glanced at Cassie, who was standing by the sink, but the redhead shrugged, appearing as clueless of what was going on as Janet was. Turning the TV on, Maria flipped through the channels until she reached a local news channel. They were reporting on some breaking news.

"Carlisle Development is facing legal repercussions after evidence of company-wide fraud and embezzlement was uncovered and turned over to police..."

Janet gasped. "Turn it up!"

Maria did so, and the three women watched as the report continued, cutting to footage of Carlisle's headquarters. People were being escorted out by the police, some in handcuffs, some not. When Janet spotted Harold being led out in cuffs, she released a shocked and excited cry.

"Look!" Cassie exclaimed, pointing at the TV. "I knew he was a snake! I knew it!"

Janet nodded, entranced by the images flashing across the screen.

"For the foreseeable future, all projects currently overseen by Carlisle Development are being brought to a halt as the company's assets are seized. This is an ongoing investigation, but officials have indicated that a compensation fund will be set up using Carlisle assets to reimburse those individuals and communities victimized and defrauded by the enterprise. We'll continue to keep you informed of the developing situation as more information is provided."

Janet couldn't believe it. She was absolutely stunned. Just like that, Carlisle Development was no longer a threat to her or her business, and she'd never have to worry about Harold walking through the store's front doors to badger and harass her ever again.

"What do you think happened?" Cassie murmured, looking at Janet with wide, shocked eyes.

Janet had a pretty good idea of what had happened. Rick Masters had happened. This had to be his doing. It'd been over a week since he'd told her he had a plan to get rid of Carlisle, and while he hadn't given her any details of what that plan was, she had no doubt this was the result of what he'd put into motion.

Besides, who else would have the resources and ability to bring down a national enterprise in the span of a week? Only a billionaire with a team of security experts at his beck and call.

"So, this means the bakery is going to be safe now,

right?" Maria asked, the relief clear in her voice. "No more graffiti or rocks through the windows?"

Janet grinned at her and nodded. "Yes, that's what this means. I think this calls for a celebration! Let's close early today and get the afternoon crew. I'll take you all out to lunch, on me!"

Both women nodded and eagerly agreed to the idea. After watching the news for a few minutes more, the three dispersed and went back to work so they could finish up for the day before lunch. Janet grabbed her cellphone, and as the others got busy, she stepped out the back door of the store into the alley and dialed Rick's number.

He answered on the second ring.

"Hey there," he said. "I was thinking I might get a call from you today."

Janet chuckled and shook her head. "Yes, well, Carlisle Development is all over the news. Seems they've run into a bit of trouble. I'm sure you had nothing to do with it, though."

"Oh, no, I totally did," he admitted with a satisfied laugh. "Honestly, it wasn't as hard as it should've been. Plenty of Carlisle employees were ready to turn on the company with the right motivation."

"Hmmm, that doesn't sound entirely ethical," she teased.

"I don't see why not," he replied cheekily. "They were going to lose their jobs when the company tanked. Now they have some emergency funds to fall back on."

"My hero," she giggled.

"I told you I'd take care of it. That I'd protect you."

Sighing, Janet leaned back against the brick wall of the bakery with a small smile.

"Yes...yes you did. I didn't doubt you for a second."

There was a moment of silence before he said, "I suppose this means you won't need my services anymore."

"I suppose I won't," she agreed. "But I'd like to thank you properly for all you've done before we end our business relationship. How's dinner at my place sound? Tonight at seven?"

"I'll be there," he promised.

"Good," she stated. "It's a date."

* * *

She was strangely nervous as she waited for Rick to arrive later that evening. This was their first, real-ish date, and she wanted everything to be perfect. She had a lasagna and a loaf of garlic bread in the oven, and was mixing a salad when the doorbell rang.

Taking in a deep breath, Janet smoothed the skirt of her lacy blue dress and made her way across the house to the front door. She opened it with a smile, and then let out a delightful gasp. Rick stood at the threshold holding a bouquet of gorgeous red velvety roses that had a slight but noticeable sweet fragrance.

Janet reached out to take them. "They're beautiful! Thank you."

"You're welcome," he told her, stepping inside when she moved to let him in. "I also brought this."

He held up a bottle of Dom Perignon, shocking her further.

"What's that for?" she asked in a breathless tone.

"We're celebrating, aren't we?" he replied with a wink. "I thought it was only appropriate."

Grinning, Janet shut the door and turned to head back

to the kitchen. "Well then, pop it open. I'll get us some glasses."

Rick did as she suggested and followed her into the kitchen before popping the cork of the champagne bottle. He poured it into the two champagne flutes she provided and they held them up in a toast.

"To you," Rick said.

"And to you," Janet replied.

They toasted with their glasses and Janet took a sip, relishing the bubbles and rich flavor as it slid down her throat.

Setting her glass down, she turned to the oven. "Dinner should be done."

She pulled out the lasagna and bread and Rick took the heavy pan from her. She grabbed the salad and followed him out to the dining room. They sat and ate and laughed together, and Janet felt all the worry and stress from the last few months simply melt away in his presence. She could hardly believe everything that had happened in such a short amount of time, and she could hardly believe that Rick Masters was sitting with her, sharing food and champagne as he gazed at her with obvious desire.

It made her giddy and excited for what was yet to come.

As they finished their meal, they continued to sit and talk about everything and nothing. Rick held her hand and told her stories from his time as a Navy Seal. His triumphs and heartbreaks, as well as some darker moments he didn't easily share with anyone. He told her about starting his company and working day and night to make it a success.

In turn, she told him about starting the bakery and how dedicated she had grown to Mountain Falls.

Before she knew it, it was nearly midnight. Rick looked at his watch and chuckled in surprise.

"Time does fly, doesn't it?" he asked, looking back up at her. "I should probably get going..."

"Wait," she said, grabbing his hand again to stop him from getting out of his chair. "Don't go. I've got something else I need to tell you."

He frowned in curiosity as he slowly sat back down.

"What is it?" he asked.

Breathing deeply, Janet held his gaze and confessed, "I love you, Rick. I've never stopped loving you...I don't expect you to feel the same..."

"But I do," Rick stated, cutting her off. "I love you too."

She was so caught off guard by his confession that she let out a surprised little cry as tears gathered in her eyes.

He chuckled. "I'm head over heels for you. I'm sorry it took me so long to acknowledge it. I've been holding back for so many reasons that just really don't matter. I want to be with you, Janet. I want to build a life with you."

Janet swallowed, fighting not to be overwhelmed by the wave of emotions washing over her. She was so happy that she could hardly breathe.

Laughing with joy, she jumped to her feet and threw her arms around his neck. He returned her embrace, bringing her lips to his. Janet poured all her feelings for him into that kiss. All her hopes and dreams for their future. As she did that, she released the last of her anger and resentment from the past. None of that mattered anymore. It didn't matter how they'd reached that point together, only that they had.

Chapter 9

Rick – 6 Months Later

He was nervous. He'd never been so nervous in his life. Even during his time in the military, he'd never felt such a soul-deep anxiety that shook his very core. It wasn't fear that was making him nervous, though. It was the excitement at the prospect of making such a life-changing decision...so long as she said yes.

Rick was preparing to propose to Janet. He'd honestly been wanting to since the night they first confessed their love for each other, but he'd decided to wait so he didn't bombard her with too much too fast.

He couldn't wait anymore, though. He wanted Janet to be his wife, and he wanted to be her husband.

Standing in the middle of her parents' backyard, he gazed over to where she stood, talking to her friend Cassie. When her mom and dad had invited them to a backyard barbecue party they were having, Rick had known it would be the perfect time to propose to her. It brought things full circle and he wanted to erase the pain of the past once and for all.

Suddenly, a hand clapped down on his shoulder, breaking him from his wandering thoughts.

"If you could stop ogling my sister, that'd be great," Evan drawled with an exaggerated sigh. "It's giving me the ick."

Chuckling, Rick shrugged Evan's hand off his shoulder and replied, "It's not my fault she's so gorgeous she scrambles my brain. I just want to ogle her all day every day."

Evan shuddered and rolled his eyes. "I knew I'd regret giving this relationship my blessing."

Rick patted him on the back in sympathy. "Even without your blessing, I'd still be with her. I just want you to know that."

Evan scowled. "I hate you sometimes, you know *that*?"

"Yes, I do. And I'm oddly okay with it."

Evan shook his head but couldn't hold back his laughter. Before he could say anything else, his mom called for him.

"I'll catch up with you later, man," Evan said before he turned to hurry away.

Rick focused his attention back on Janet and decided he couldn't wait any longer, as he patted his front pocket to make sure the ring was still safely tucked away there. Taking a deep breath, he crossed the yard toward her. She caught his eye as he approached and her expression lit up, her smile growing wider.

When he reached her, he put his hand on the small of her back and pressed a kiss to her forehead.

"Hey there," she said, grinning up at him.

"Hey," he replied with a smile. "Can I steal you a second?"

She arched her brows in surprise, but nodded.

Glancing toward Cassie, she asked, "We'll be right back."

Cassie nodded, shooting Rick a knowing look. "All right. Don't wander off too far you two."

She gave Rick a wink as she passed by him. Janet didn't seem to notice, though. Rick took her hand.

"Come with me," he said before leading her to the trees surrounding the yard.

"Where are we going?" she asked with a laugh.

"I need to show you something," he told her.

When they reached the small clearing beneath the treehouse, he stopped and faced her. She looked around with a frown.

"What are we doing here?" she asked, her tone hesitant. "The last time we were here together..."

"I know," he nodded. "I want to erase that memory from your mind and replace it with something new."

She gave him a cautious smile. "Okay...I don't know what's going on in that head of yours, but I trust you, Rick."

Taking her hands in his, he said, "Janet, I know the last time we were here, things didn't end so well. I hurt you, and I'll forever be sorry for that. I was confused and short-sighted back then, but I don't think we were ready for each other yet. In the years since then, we've both grown and matured. I think we're finally the people we've needed to be for each other."

Her expression softened and the caution left her gaze.

"I agree," she softly said with a nod. "As much as your rejection hurt back then, I was too young. I wasn't ready, and I love you more now than I could've thought possible back then."

His heart swelled at that. She was way too good for him.

"I love you so much, I can't imagine my life without

you," he continued. As she watched him, he pulled the velvet box from his pocket and lowered to one knee.

Janet's eyes widened with shock. "Rick...what are you doing?"

He held the box out to her, opening it to reveal a diamond ring that Cassie had helped him pick out. Janet gasped, covering her mouth with her hands as she gazed down at him.

"Janet, I love you with all my heart," Rick said. "You are the most beautiful, brilliant, and wonderful person I have ever known. I want to spend the rest of my life with you, and I hope you feel the same. At the risk of sounding cheesy, would you make me the happiest man in the world and marry me?"

Tears instantly began running down her cheeks and a shuddering sob broke past her lips. Rick felt a moment of uncertainty when she didn't respond for several moments, but when she dropped her hands from her mouth, he could see she was smiling.

"Yes!" she exclaimed. "Yes, of course I'll marry you!"

A breath of relief rushed out of Rick and he grabbed her hand, taking the ring out of its box and sliding it on her finger.

Pushing to his feet, he scooped her up into his arms and spun her around in the air as he kissed her. Janet wrapped her arms around his neck and clung to him, crying and laughing between their kisses.

When he set her back down on the ground, she stared up at him with love and happiness shining in her eyes.

Before he could say anything more to her, though, the air was filled with the sound of clapping and cheering. Surprised, he turned to find Evan, Cassie, and pretty much everyone else from the party watching them with looks of excitement.

"It's about time!" Evan called.

"I'm sorry, Rick," Cassie said with a laugh. "I couldn't help myself!"

Rick grinned at her and shook his head.

"It's fine," he told her. "At least you didn't let it slip beforehand."

The crowd of people moved toward them, shouts of congratulations and well-wishes surrounding them. Rick hugged Janet's parents before Evan found him and they shook hands.

"Congratulations, buddy," Evan declared with a grin. "Just make sure she's happy, all right?"

Rick nodded. "Absolutely."

That would be his life's main mission.

Separated by the crowd, Rick and Janet were bounced from one person to another as everyone clamored for their attention. Eventually, they managed to find their way back to each other.

"All right, everyone!" Janet's dad exclaimed. "Let's go back and I'll break out the champagne so we can really celebrate!"

He turned and led the rest of the party back towards the backyard, along with Evan and Cassie.

Alone again, Rick released a long breath.

"For the record, that wasn't part of my plan."

Smiling, Janet slipped into his arms and gazed up at him.

"It's all right," she assured him. "I actually kind of liked sharing that moment with my family and Cassie...as well as all my parents' neighbors."

Rick grinned at her teasing tone.

"Well, as long as you're happy, I consider it a success," he murmured.

"I love you," she told him, her tone heavy with emotion. "I cannot wait to spend the rest of my life with you."

"I love you too," he replied with as much conviction as her. "I swear, I'll do whatever I have to in order to make you happy. You are my everything, Janet. I didn't understand that ten years ago, but I do now, and I'm not going to waste another moment of my life without you by my side."

Ten years ago, Rick had turned her away, too overwhelmed and unprepared for her love and adoration. Now, he would spend the rest of his life earning every moment she gave him of both...and he knew it would be a life he would cherish until the moment it ended.

Made in the USA
Las Vegas, NV
17 January 2024